Jacob chased after the ball and got it. He turned to get a shot, but the fullback had come over to take him.

The guy reached in and knocked the ball away.

Jacob dashed back to the ball, but he was guarded closely now.

And Brian, who had come all the way up the field from his sweeper position, surged past his defender. Jacob slid a little pass across the grass to him.

Brian, like a forward, whipped his leg at the ball, hit it with his shoelaces, and *drove* it at the goal.

Books about the kids from Angel Park:

Angel Park All-Stars

Angel Park Soccer Stars

ANGEL PARK
SOCCER STARS
6

TOTAL SOCCER

By Dean Hughes

Illustrated by Dennis Lyall

Bullseye Books • Alfred A. Knopf
New York

Library of Congress Cataloging-in-Publication Data
Hughes, Dean, 1943–
Total soccer / by Dean Hughes ; illustrated by Dennis Lyall.
p.   cm. — (Angel Park soccer stars ; 6)
Summary: The Angel Park Pride must learn to play not as a group of
talented individuals, but as a single unit, if they are to win the
championship.
ISBN 0-679-82635-1 (pbk.) — ISBN 0-679-92635-6 (lib. bdg.)
[1. Soccer—Fiction.]   I. Lyall, Dennis, ill.   II. Title.
III. Series: Hughes, Dean, 1943– Angel Park soccer stars ; 6.
PZ7.H87312To 1992 [Fic]—dc20   91-25420
RL: 4.4
First Bullseye Books edition: June 1992

Manufactured in the United States of America
10 9 8 7 6 5 4 3 2 1

for Bobby Boyd

★1★

No Problem!

═══════════════════════

Jacob Scott was staying tight on a Desert Palm fullback. The Angel Park team was way ahead of the Gila Monsters, but that didn't matter to Jacob. He liked to play all out— and keep the pressure on the guy he was marking.

Jacob saw a pass coming. He broke ahead and outran the fullback—a guy named Rowley—to the ball.

But Rowley didn't give up. He stepped in and tried to steal the ball back.

That was a big mistake. Jacob pushed the ball right under Rowley's reaching foot. Then he slipped around, took control of the ball, and broke free.

Clayton Lindsay had seen the whole thing coming. Clayton was from England, and he was by far the best player on the team. He charged back toward the goal. He had to slow down enough to let a defender pass him—so he wouldn't be offside. But he was in a good spot.

Jacob kicked a high pass. Clayton leaped and turned in the air. He cradled the ball against his middle and let it drop to the ground.

At the same time Jacob ran straight at the goal. Clayton's defender saw what was coming. Jacob was in the clear—with no one to stop him except the goalie.

So the defender left Clayton and charged at Jacob.

Clayton kicked the ball out to . . . no, he faked!

Then he spun around and faced Johnny Syme, the goalie, who had no help at all.

Clayton looked left and fired right.

Syme was left frozen.

The ball caught the net for another goal. The score was now 8 to 1.

The Pride was wiping out the poor Desert Palm Gila Monsters.

And Clayton was enjoying it. "Hey, Syme," he yelled, "did you even *see* that one go by?"

Clayton was breaking Coach Toscano's rule by yelling stuff like that. The coach didn't mind celebrating, but he was strictly against any kind of taunting.

Heidi Wells said, "Hey, come on, Clayton, don't start that." Heidi always encouraged everyone to have a good attitude.

Clayton paid no attention. He trotted down the field, laughing and joking with Billy Bacon. Jacob heard Billy say, "I don't think these guys are worse than they were when we played them the first time. We're just a *whole lot* better."

Jacob thought that might be true. Still, Billy was talking loudly enough for everyone to hear—the Gila Monsters and even the parents on the sidelines. *And* Billy was one of the weakest players. Jacob didn't think that kind of bragging sounded good.

Things got even worse when Adam Snarr trotted onto the field to substitute for Brian Rohatinsky. Adam wasn't any superstar, but he was bragging, too. He yelled to Billy, "Hey, this is my chance. *Anyone* can score on this goalie."

Billy yelled back, "He can't help it. He's just a little slow, that's all."

Coach Toscano heard the boys this time. He shouted, "That's enough of that stuff. Let's just play soccer!"

Jacob was glad to hear that. He was also happy to see his friend Nate Matheson come onto the field as goalie. Nate had sprained his ankle a couple of weeks before. For the most part he had sat on the sidelines and shouted instructions to the new back-up goalie, Jared Trajillo. His ankle was still giving him some trouble.

"How does the ankle feel?" Jacob yelled to him.

"Good. I'll be okay."

And he *was* okay.

Jimmy Archibald fired a shot right after Nate got into the game. He hit the ball low and hard. Nate dove and grabbed it with both hands. Then he jumped up and kicked a good "outlet" pass to the wing.

That was a good sign. His ankle seemed fine.

And then a little more misery came to the Desert Palm team.

Harrison, their right wing, got faked by

Henry White, and he fell down. Henry was fast, and he darted toward the goal. Musselman, a forward for the Gila Monsters, came over to cut off Henry.

He tried a sliding tackle, but Henry saw it coming. He pulled up and let Musselman slide across the grass.

Then Henry shot forward and flipped a pass into the air.

Clayton tried to get up for a header, but he was blocked. A defender knocked the ball away.

But everything was working for the Pride today. Heidi raced toward the ball and so did the goalie. But the ball took a sideways bounce right to Heidi.

She slammed it past the goalie and into the net.

9 to 1.

Jacob slapped hands with Heidi. He had to admit it was fun to rip a team apart this way.

Still, he did feel kind of sorry for the Gila Monsters. And he was embarrassed when he heard Clayton shout to Billy, "This isn't a win. This is a *massacre!*"

At least the match ended soon after that.

And the Gila Monsters were good enough sports to line up and slap hands with the Pride—without saying too much.

That seemed to shut up Clayton and Billy for a time. But when the players all walked over to the side of the field, the two started again.

"*No one* can beat us now," Clayton told some of the players. "Nate's back and looking good. And our attack is clicking like a machine. We're going to tear up the Springers."

"Hey, what about the Racers?" Jacob said.

Everyone turned and looked at him.

"What about them?" Clayton asked.

"We play them on Thursday. That's the team we have to think about right now."

"We've beaten them *twice* this year," Brian said.

"That's right. And they were both tough matches, weren't they?"

"The Racers are good," Heidi said. "We can't look past them."

"I'm not looking past anyone," Clayton said. "I plan to make Gerstein look silly. I'm going to score so many goals he'll never open that big mouth of his again."

Some of the players liked that. No one could stand Gerstein. Billy shouted, *"Yeah!"* And then so did Adam and Brian.

By then the coach had walked up. "Sit down, kids," he said.

Jacob hoped Coach Toscano had heard some of the stuff Clayton had been saying.

But the coach said, "Well, players, what I saw out there today was pretty close to 'total soccer.' Everyone played defense, and everyone was part of the attack. That's what we've been trying to do all year."

Jacob felt good about all that. He knew the team really had played well together.

"But kids," Coach Toscano added, "I heard something at the end of the match that I don't want to hear again."

He looked around at all the players.

"You know what I'm talking about. You know how much you hate it when some of the teams around the league score a goal and then rub it in. That's not soccer. That's not sportsmanship. And it shouldn't ever be part of the game."

The kids were quiet now.

"Is that understood? No more of it, all right?"

The players nodded.

"Clayton? Billy? Did you hear me?"

"Yes."

"Yes."

"All right then. Let's plan on—"

"Coach?" Jacob said.

"Yes."

"I think there's another problem. It's easy to start thinking we can wipe everybody out now. But I think the Racers will be tough."

"Of course they will. Do you think Gerstein and those kids want to lose to you three times this year? They're going to play their best match of the season. That's my guess."

"So let's be ready," Heidi said.

And Nate added, "I'm not sure my ankle is healed quite one hundred percent. And Jared still hasn't played a lot at goalie, so we need to play great defense."

"I'm glad to hear you talk that way," Coach Toscano said. "I not only heard some taunting today, I heard some bragging. Believing in ourselves is great. But we can't start thinking we're so good all we have to do is show up to win. We still have some very tough matches left."

Jacob felt a lot better.

For a few minutes.

The coach walked away, and Clayton looked over at Jacob and said, "Oh, Jacob, aren't you the coach's little pet? 'Gee, Mr. Toscano, the Racers are going to be *sooooo* tough to beat.' "

"Shut up, Clayton," Heidi said. "Jacob's right."

"Oh, I know. You and Nate and Jacob all have such *wonderful* attitudes. We all admire you *so much*. But the rest of us are going to go out there and put them away—and not worry about our *attitudes*."

"Come on, Clayton," Nate said. "Let's not divide up the team. Let's just think about playing our best against—"

"That's *just exactly* what I plan to do," Clayton said. And he got up and walked away.

Jacob didn't like the feeling that was left behind. He hoped the team wasn't heading for a letdown.

★2★

One-Man Team

That night Jacob got a call from Heidi. "You're not going to believe what I'm going to tell you," she said.

"Okay, I don't believe you," Jacob said.

"But it's true, birdbrain."

"What is?"

"What I'm going to tell you."

"So tell me."

"Why should I? You're not going to believe me."

"Okay. Okay. I believe you."

"Believe what?"

"Heidi! Lay off. Just tell me."

"Okay. Get ready." She paused to build suspense, and then she said slowly, "The Springers and the Kickers *both* lost today. We're all alone . . . in *first place!*"

"You're *kidding!*" Jacob said.

"I told you that you wouldn't believe me."

"No, I do. But I just . . . can't believe it."

"Well, it happened. We're a game ahead of the Kickers and *three* ahead of the Springers. But you know who beat the Springers—it was the Racers."

"Ugh," Jacob said, and suddenly he wasn't quite as excited. "Boy, those guys are going to be tough. If we lose, we'd be right back in a tie with the Kickers."

"That's right."

"Man, oh, man. I hope all this cocky stuff stops. We've got to have our heads on straight and play the way we did today."

"I know," Heidi said. "When the season started, we didn't have any confidence. But now some of the guys are getting *overconfident.*"

"Yeah, that's right."

And that's what Jacob thought about in bed that night. He really wanted to win the championship. But Clayton was the player who had the most influence on the team. Why couldn't the guy keep his attitude straight for more than a week at a time? What was wrong with him anyway?

When Thursday came, Gerstein was the first one to start the mouthy stuff. But Clayton and Billy jumped right into it.

"No way do you beat us three times, Lindsay," Gerstein told Clayton. "Maybe we can't win the championship now, but we can knock you out—just like we did the Springers."

Clayton, who was much taller than Gerstein, looked down his nose at him. Then he said to Billy, "Did you hear something? It sounded like some little kid trying to talk big."

"Yeah," Billy said, "I thought I heard something too. I know I can *smell* something. But it couldn't be anything big enough to worry about."

Gerstein, who was every bit as tall as Billy, stepped up close to him. "How about we find out right now how big I am, huh, Bacon? Huh, Billy Bacon?"

At least Clayton didn't let that get started. "We'll show you on the *field*, Gerstein," he said. "So get ready to feel about two inches high."

"Yeah, we'll see about that," Gerstein said, and he walked away.

Billy and Clayton both laughed. "Let's *de-*

stroy those guys!" Clayton yelled to all the Pride players.

Everyone cheered.

Jacob hoped for the best. He hoped all this cocky talk wouldn't backfire.

As it turned out, however, Clayton played like a lion. He was all over the middle of the field. He was so quick on his feet, so balanced, he could stop the Cactus Hills attack almost by himself.

And when he took over the ball, look out! He was really coming hard today.

It wasn't long before Gerstein had very little to say.

Early in the match, Clayton took a pass from Lian Jie and dribbled the ball into Racers' territory. He faked the guy who was marking him, and then he drove for the goal.

Two defenders came out to take him on. But he looked away, faked a pass, and then cut between the defenders.

Another fullback came at him. Clayton should have passed off to Jacob, who was wide open. But Clayton made a fake, and then broke past the fullback.

He drove straight at the goalie. When the goalie charged him, he snapped a *blazing* shot right past the guy's legs.

Slam!

The Pride was up 1 to 0.

Clayton spun toward Jacob and yelled, "Now are you worried? Is my *attitude* okay?"

"Nice shot" was all that Jacob said.

But Clayton seemed to read his mind. "I wanted that one myself," he said. "That's why I didn't pass to you. But the next one is yours."

"Clayton, I don't want to—"

"Hey, just get ready. I'll get the ball to you."

And he did.

A couple of minutes later he brought the ball up the middle the same way. Two defenders took him on. And then a third tried to sneak in on him. But Clayton managed to shake loose long enough to knock a pass to Jacob.

Clayton had pulled the defense to the right side. Jacob was in the middle, in front of the goal area. He pushed forward and then, when the goalie committed toward him, he slipped a pass to Heidi, on the left side.

She shot the ball home and it was 2 to 0.

"Why didn't you take it, Jacob?" Clayton said. "That one was supposed to be yours."

"She was open," Jacob said. He knew he

might have gotten the goal, had he shot. But Heidi had been in a better spot.

"Now I have to get you another one," Clayton said.

"Let's just hit the person who's open," Jacob told him.

"We can do whatever we want against these guys," Clayton answered. "Let's *show* them." And then he turned to Gerstein, who was walking away. "What's the matter, Jimmy boy, nothing to say today?"

Gerstein kept walking. He didn't say a word. Jacob couldn't help taking a little pleasure in that. But Clayton was acting the way Gerstein usually did. And that was nothing to be proud of.

Still, Clayton didn't stop playing soccer. He was going hard. The next chance he got, he fought for the ball, controlled it, and then drove toward the goal again.

He passed off to Chris Baca, but then he yelled for a pass back.

When he got it, he cut the ball behind his left foot and danced to the side. Then he darted toward the goal. And just as suddenly, he stopped.

He blasted a long shot that hit a fullback's shoulder and rebounded high in the air.

But who was there when it came down? Clayton himself.

He outjumped everyone and headed the ball past the goalie and into the net.

He leaped in the air and cheered. Then he spun around and laughed. "I should get an assist *and* a goal," he yelled to Billy.

"You should be your own cheerleader, too," Gerstein said.

But that didn't bother Clayton. "No, Gerstein. You cheer for me. I *know* you admire the way I play." When he was being really cocky, his English accent seemed the strongest.

"Nice job!" Jacob said, and he meant it.

But Clayton said, "Hey, don't worry. You'll still get your goal. I just couldn't wait for you to get open that time. You have to move a little faster if you're going to stay with me."

Jacob didn't say anything. He turned and walked down the field. He didn't want to listen to that kind of stuff.

But Jacob had to admit, Clayton was spectacular. He was all over the field. He was winning the game by himself. Maybe he bragged, but he did back it up with some real play.

When halftime came the score was still 3 to 0.

The coach had the kids sit down. Jacob had never seen him look so serious. He pushed his hands down in his pockets and just looked at the kids for a time. Finally he said, "I've never been quite so worried about our team."

He let that sink in for a long time. He had everyone's attention. Jacob watched Clayton, and he could see that Clayton knew what was coming. He already looked angry.

"One great player, on a certain day, can rise up and almost win a match by himself," he said. "But in the long run, championships cannot be won that way. No one, not even Pelé, could ever carry a team alone."

"Clayton's just playing good today," Billy said. "What does that hurt?"

"Playing well doesn't hurt anything," Coach Toscano said. But then he looked straight at Clayton. "But we are a team. When defenders know that *anyone* on our team might score, they have to be honest in guarding every one of us. That's what total soccer is all about. When one player moves into an attack position, another rotates back to cover on defense. But Clayton, that means you have to let others make their moves— and that's when you can drop back and take defenders with you. If you're always the shooter, the whole defense pulls in on you."

He stopped and took a long look at Clayton, and then he added, "For the last couple of weeks we've played as a *unit*. That's more important to me than winning the championship."

Clayton's face was burning. Jacob knew how mad he was.

"Do you understand that, Clayton?"

"Yes," Clayton said, and that was all.

"All right," Coach Toscano said. "Clayton, I want you to know I'm proud of you. You're a great player, and you played your heart out. All I'm asking is that you play *with* your teammates."

Clayton nodded, but he still looked angry.

"Okay, players," the coach said. "Get a drink and rest. But let's be ready to play team soccer when we go back on the field."

That's when Jacob heard what Clayton said to Billy. "Fine. I'll let everyone else do the shooting—and we'll see how great the team is."

That was not at all what the coach meant, and Clayton knew it. But Jacob didn't dare say anything.

★ 3 ★

Comeback

====================

Clayton changed the way he played in the second half. He marked his man. But he didn't work hard and didn't fight for the ball.

And every time Clayton got the ball, he passed off. Then he trotted down the field. He did nothing to make the attack work.

Jacob knew exactly what Clayton was doing. He was saying, "Okay, see how well you can play without me?"

And the Pride did not play well.

The defense held together, but the attack was dead.

Then the defense started to lose its edge. Trenton Daynes and Tanya Gardner were playing now, and they just weren't as tough on defense as they needed to be. Jared was playing goalie now so that Nate wouldn't overwork his bad ankle. And Jared still made rookie mistakes at times.

When Gerstein tried a long shot that arched toward the goal, Jared should have gone out to meet it. But he stayed back and waited. The Racers' big forward saw the chance. He turned a long, weak shot into a good pass.

He headed the ball into the net for the Racers' first goal.

"Don't count us out *yet!*" Gerstein shouted. He looked over at Clayton, as if he expected some sort of answer.

Instead, Clayton walked away. Jacob ran over to him. "Come on, Clayton. The coach didn't mean that you should stop playing. He just said to play *with* the team."

"I would, Jacob, but I don't have your wonderful attitude."

"Clayton, don't do this. We need you to play hard. He just meant that you shouldn't take the ball all the way down the field and shoot it, too. You should pass off."

"As I recall, I passed off to you and gave you a good chance to score—if you had only taken it."

"Clayton, you know what you were doing. You—"

"Leave me alone, Jacob. You guys are all great—just like the coach says. I'll just *fit in* and be part of the team."

He walked away.

And from that point he did even less. He avoided the ball, and he did very little on defense.

The Racers could feel the difference, and they were pressing. The left wing took a short punt from the goalie and headed it forward to a midfielder. The midfielder shot a good lead pass to Gerstein.

Gerstein got doubled by Sterling Malone and Tammy Hill, but he managed to nudge the ball into the middle of the field.

That was Clayton's area, and he normally would have been there. But he made no move to the ball.

That's when a midfielder moved up, took the ball, and dribbled forward. Then he dropped the ball back to Gerstein.

Gerstein took a long shot that Sterling blocked. But the ball rolled into the goal area, and a Racers' forward got to it first. He knocked it in for goal number two.

Jacob looked around for Clayton. He was the one who always got to the loose balls. But this time he was well away from the action.

He stood with his hands on his hips. He shrugged, and he cocked his head to one side, as if to say, "Well, you got what you deserved."

Just then Coach Toscano shouted, "Clayton, come off the field. Tanya is going to play for you."

Clayton spun around. He looked shocked. Jacob walked a little closer, and he heard the coach say, "You would rather make a point than win this match, wouldn't you?"

Clayton said, "No, I . . ." But he stopped, and he never finished his sentence. He looked very angry.

Coach Toscano also sent Nate back onto the field. And the Pride got ready to play some big-time defense.

And they did.

Without Clayton, they were not the same team. But they played well together. They marked their own players, and they covered for one another, falling off and doubling when they could.

They were careful not to get caught out of position—maybe too careful. They were slow to switch to their attack. And when they did move into attack, they didn't have the same power without Clayton in the middle.

Jacob had the feeling that the Pride players would have to rely on good defense, and he hoped they could hold the lead. As the match got closer to the end, the chances of doing that looked pretty good.

But their luck didn't hold out.

Henry, who was normally very tough on defense, gambled a little on a tackle and got beat. The wing got loose for a breakaway and drove straight at Nate.

Nate, still favoring his ankle, was a little too careful. He came out to meet the wing, but he didn't charge as hard as he usually would.

The wing had just enough time to get the

angle he needed. He drove his shot before Nate could go for the ball.

It skidded just inside the goalpost for a score.

Now the Racers really did go nuts. The match that had looked like a runaway was now tied up.

Gerstein ran to the sideline and shouted at Clayton, "Hey, Lindsay, where were you when your team needed you? You're a *loser*."

Clayton didn't say a word.

Jacob had no idea what he was thinking now.

But the coach walked over to him and said something, and then Clayton ran back on the field. Jacob knew that Coach Toscano had tried to teach him a lesson. What he hoped was that Clayton had gotten the point.

One thing soon became clear: Clayton didn't want to lose. He played hard when he came back on the field.

He went after a midfielder and took the ball. Then he zipped right past the guy and headed up the field.

Jacob hoped he would work the ball and make sure someone got a good shot. But it soon became obvious that that was not what he had in mind.

He was going after the goal himself—all over again.

He dribbled and cut, faked, slowed, then burst forward. He kept working against his man—one-on-one. He made his way through the middle, even though other players were closing in on him.

When he finally drew in defenders from all sides, he was forced to try a pass. But a fullback got in the way, and the ball hit him and then bounded back up the field.

Now Clayton's quickness paid off. He jumped past a defender and darted to the ball. But instead of controlling it and turning, he dropped it behind him with the sole of his shoe. Then he spun and broke back between two defenders toward the goal.

He was suddenly in open space, and so he drove hard. When a fullback came up to take him, Jacob was suddenly wide open for a shot. But Clayton didn't take a look. He took on the fullback, feinted and drove, and then nudged a surprise shot off to the side.

The shot slipped in front of the goalie and

barely caught the corner of the net—just inside the goalpost.

Just like that! He had done it. The Pride had the lead again.

And they didn't let go.

Clayton played like a wild man. He took over the middle of the field.

And just before the match ended, he slammed home another goal.

But as soon as the match was over, he walked off the field and straight across the park.

Jacob hated to see him do that. Somehow, the team needed to get back together.

So Jacob ran and caught up with Clayton. "Clayton, stay around. The coach wants to talk to us—like always.'"

"The coach already *talked* to me. I've heard enough for one day. If I had done what he told me, we would have lost the match."

"Clayton, all he was trying to tell you was that—"

"I know what he said. And I showed what I can do. I want to win the championship. And if I have to, I'll do it by myself."

"Clayton, that won't work. I don't see why you—"

"Jacob, was your dad at the game today?"

"What?"

"You heard me."

"Yeah, he was there."

"What would he say to you if we had lost today?"

Jacob couldn't see what Clayton was getting at. "I don't know," he said.

" 'Tough luck. Good luck next time.' Something like that. Right?" Clayton wiped the sweat off his forehead and pushed his long hair back. His face was very red.

"Yeah. I guess so."

"Then don't talk to me. You don't know what I'm up against." And then he turned and walked away.

Jacob just stood there. He had no idea what Clayton was trying to say.

★ 4 ★

Conflict

On Saturday morning the Pride got together to practice. Jacob wondered whether Clayton would even show up.

But he did, and he seemed to be in a good mood. He got to the park early, sat down, and started putting on his soccer shoes. The coach hadn't arrived yet.

Jacob thought this was his chance to patch things up with Clayton. The team didn't need a lot of bad feelings right now—not with the championship on the line.

"Clayton," Jacob said, "I'm sorry about what happened on Thursday. All I meant was—"

"Don't worry about it, Scott," Clayton said. "It doesn't matter now, anyway. All we have to do is beat the Springers on Monday and we've got it. And the Springers are falling apart."

Jacob knew what Clayton meant. The Springers had lost to the Bandits on Thursday. That was two losses in a row for them, and they just weren't playing well. "Yeah, but you know how much they'll want to beat us."

"I don't care how much they *want* to beat us. I say they *can't*."

Jacob thought maybe he better let the whole thing drop. He didn't want to get an argument started again.

Jacob took a step away, but Clayton said, "What's the matter, Jacob? Do I have the wrong *attitude* again? Just because I believe we can win?"

Billy had just walked up. "Yeah, you're supposed to think we'll lose. That's how Jacob likes to think."

"No, I don't," Jacob said, and now he was getting angry. "But the Springers are good. They may not be playing very well right now. But they can. We've *seen* how good they can be."

"Hey, I don't know what you're worried about. I played hard against the Racers."

"I know you played hard, Clayton. But you hogged the ball, and you played too much one-on-one."

"Yeah, well, what was the score when I was playing things my way? And what was the score when I stopped?"

Most of the players were there now. They had all stopped what they were doing. As Clayton and Jacob's voices had risen, everyone was watching and listening. Jacob didn't like what was happening.

"Look, Clayton, I don't want to—"

"You tell me how we got three goals ahead, and then how we lost that lead. And then you tell me who won the game for us."

Jacob's temper flashed all over again. "That's because you quit *playing*. That's not what the coach asked you to do. That's *stupid*."

Clayton reached out and grabbed Jacob by the shirt. Maybe he would have punched Jacob if he hadn't heard the coach yell, "Hey, boys, what's going on?"

Clayton let go as the coach walked up to

the boys. "Nothing," he said. "We were just messing around." He tried to smile.

But the coach knew better. "We've got the championship game on Monday. How can we play good soccer if you guys are fighting with each other?"

"I'm sorry, Coach," Clayton said. "But don't worry. We'll win."

"Clayton, I'd rather lose than have you win the game by yourself. I've talked all year about total soccer—a whole team working together. And just when we had almost gotten to that point, you made up your mind to do things your own way."

Clayton didn't answer. He put his hands on his hips and looked down at the ground.

"Play hard. But play together," the coach said.

"Okay," Clayton said.

But Jacob didn't like what he saw in practice. During a three-on-three drill, Clayton watched some of his teammates. "I can't wait to show Robbie Jackson who's the best around here," he told some of the players. Jackson was the Springers' big star. He pointed at the players doing the drill—mostly younger players. "I wouldn't want to rely on *them* to win the match."

But then he noticed that Jacob had heard him. "Scott, don't worry your little head," he said. "We'll beat the Springers—easy."

Jacob couldn't believe it. Clayton still hadn't really heard the coach.

And that was obvious when Monday came around.

Clayton was still bragging and talking big. Before the game, he told Robbie Jackson, "You better be ready. I'm going to show you what I've got today."

Jackson smiled. "Give it your best shot," he said. And somehow Jacob saw more real confidence in Jackson than he did in Clayton. Jacob couldn't figure out why Clayton thought he had to talk so big. As good as he was, Clayton shouldn't have to brag.

As soon as the match with the Springers began, one thing was clear. That team had come to play. They had no chance for the championship now, but they wanted to end the season with some pride—by beating the Pride.

The guy guarding Jacob was right on top of him every second, and so were the other defenders. Jacob just hoped they would wear down in time.

What was even more scary was that

Jackson was going at Clayton hard, using all his moves. And then there was Metzger, the Springers' great forward. He looked as if he meant business today, too.

When Clayton played against a team like the Racers—without a defender who could stay with him—he could do almost anything he wanted. But Jackson was a hard-nosed defender, very quick and very smart. Clayton's moves didn't fool him.

And coming the other way, on attack, Jackson could give Clayton all he could handle.

The worst part was, the Springers were twice as intense as the Pride. In the early minutes they took advantage of that. The ball was usually on the Pride defensive end of the field. And Jackson kept working hard.

For a while the Pride defense kept him from getting off too many dangerous shots. Nate pulled down the ones he did get off.

Halfway through the first half, Jackson raced in and controlled a loose ball. Clayton was right with him, and he marked him well. Jackson spun so he was facing the goal, and Clayton was with him nose-to-nose.

That's when Clayton decided to make a

steal. He stepped in close and tried to kick the ball. But Jackson had seen that move coming. He pulled back just in time, and he spotted Metzger breaking for the goal area.

With Clayton off-balance, Jackson hammered a pass right past him. Metzger leaped up and kicked the ball before it ever touched the ground. It was a bang-bang play, and Nate didn't have time to react in the goal.

Whoosh!

The ball shot past Nate and zinged against the strings of the net.

The Springers cheered, and Clayton stomped away.

Jacob hoped that maybe now the Pride players would wake up. The Springers had come to play, and all that talk about them falling apart hadn't done one bit of good.

Now it was Clayton who was telling everyone, "Okay, let's get after 'em. We can't let these guys take our championship away."

But the Springers were playing with confidence now. And Angel Park just wasn't clicking.

Jacob watched Clayton try to take over the match, but he couldn't do it against Jackson. When he tried to get by the guy, he lost the ball or he got bogged down.

The team needed quick, sharp passes, not show-off plays by Clayton. But the harder Clayton shouted encouragement to the team, the more he relied on himself.

The Springers could see what was happening. They could double Clayton almost any time they wanted since he would only pass the ball when he absolutely had to.

And the more he got stripped of the ball, the more he tried the next time to prove he could dribble his way through.

Coach Toscano kept shouting to Clayton that he needed to work with the team, but Clayton hardly seemed to notice.

And then his dribbling in a crowd backfired on him—big time.

Jackson was marking Clayton as he took the ball across the field and looked for an opening. As Clayton tried to put a move on Jackson, he didn't notice that a midfielder had come around his blind side.

The midfielder stole the ball and then gave it a good kick upfield.

The Springers got a big jump on the Pride defenders, and they broke up the field, three-on-two.

Metzger took the middle. He passed off the ball to the right, got it back, and went to the left—and then back to the right again. The three ran hard but didn't dribble much. They kept Sterling and Tammy guessing.

And then, as they neared the goal area where Nate could even up the odds, they didn't get too anxious.

Metzger had a possible shot, but Sterling was on him tight. He faked the shot and then flipped the ball over to the girl who played the right wing.

She pulled back her leg to take a shot, but then she dropped the ball right back to Metzger. Sterling didn't get too far out of position, but he had taken one step toward the wing when she faked the shot.

It was all the room Metzger needed.

He fired the ball hard past Nate.

2 to 0!

And Clayton, who was just catching up to the play, yelled, "What are you doing, Sterling? Can't you even mark that guy?"

That's when the coach pulled Clayton off the field.

★ 5 ★

Too Late?

With Clayton off the field, the Pride didn't get any better. The attack lost a lot of speed when he wasn't out there. And the defense needed someone who could stay with Jackson.

So the game turned into a stand-off. Without Clayton hogging the ball, Angel Park began to get more shots. But they didn't score. Neither did the Springers.

At halftime the score was still 2 to 0.

When the players came to the side of the field, Jacob noticed that Clayton didn't look so cocky anymore. Or maybe he was just sad because he didn't want to lose the game. Either way, he wasn't saying much.

The coach talked to the players about teamwork again, and then he took Clayton aside. The two had a long talk. Clayton didn't seem to be arguing. Maybe that was a good sign.

When the second half started, Clayton was back on the field. And he wasn't dribbling so much. He was trying to pass off and work with the other players.

Jacob could feel that the attack was starting to move better. Maybe they still had a chance. The only problem was, the Angel Park players were too anxious to make up for the first half.

Jacob himself took a shot when he should have worked the ball in closer. And Heidi had a good chance to head in a shot, but she tried to put too much on the ball, and it sailed high over the goal.

The match turned into a hard battle, with lots of banging and tough defense. But neither team could get much going.

The Pride kept pushing and pressuring, however, and something finally turned their way.

The Springers had a throw-in from the

touchline. Henry guessed where the ball was going, and he slipped in quickly and stole the throw.

He timed his break just right, and he was suddenly flying down the touchline with no one near him.

As he veered toward the goal a midfielder caught up with him, but Henry kept right on going. Jacob turned on his speed and chased the play.

Henry still had the advantage, so he drove a hard shot at the goal. The goalie jumped to his left and just barely got a hand on the ball.

The ball bounced away, and that's when Jacob's hard run paid off. He was right there when the ball bounced toward him.

His instincts told him to shoot the ball hard and low, and by now his practice had paid off. He hit the ball with the side of his foot, lashed it hard, bringing his knee through first. The ball stayed down and slashed past the goalie.

2 to 1!

Finally, the Pride had something going. They could pull out this championship yet.

Clayton ran to Jacob and Henry. He slapped them both on the backs. "All right. Let's get another one. These guys aren't that tough."

Jacob didn't know what to think of that. It was a strange thing to say, considering how the match had gone so far. Still, Clayton was trying to work with the team now.

The whole Angel Park team seemed to turn up their intensity after that first goal.

They pressed hard on defense, and they moved the ball well on attack. Clayton seemed to realize that what he had been doing earlier hadn't worked, and he wasn't trying to dominate.

Then Jackson pulled a slick one. He came straight at Clayton, faked a pass but stepped over the ball. At the same time he broke to his right and left the ball behind.

Metzger, who was coming up behind, took the ball in the clear, and burst down the middle. When Tammy came over to mark him, he powered a shot on goal.

The shot was low and to Nate's right. That's where he had been weak since his injury. But he reacted quickly this time. He dove for the ball, caught it, and pulled it in.

Then he hopped up and looked for a teammate. He saw Clayton waving for the ball. He kicked him a good pass.

The whole team seemed to be fired up by Nate's save. They switched quickly to attack and went hard.

Clayton dribbled only a short way before two defenders closed on him. But that left Lian open. Clayton led Lian with a nice pass.

Lian made a good run into Springer territory before the defense closed on him. He quickly dropped the ball over to Chris Baca, on the wing. Chris took the ball along the touchline. Then he turned and kicked it back to Lian.

Lian didn't hold the ball. He controlled it and shot it right back to the middle of the field. But Jackson saw the ball heading for Clayton and went after it.

Jackson and Clayton got to the ball at the same time. Each got a foot on it. The ball shot in the air and off to one side. Clayton leaped and stretched out parallel to the ground.

He got a foot on the ball and hit it upfield, but he couldn't get it to one of his players.

A Springer fullback went after the ball, but Heidi had more speed. She outran the guy and, without ever controlling the ball, kicked it to Jacob.

Jacob had the ball in front of the goal area. He didn't want to waste a wild shot.

As Jacob looked to his right, the defender dropped back a little, ready to block a shot. Jacob suddenly surprised him. He nudged the ball straight past the guy and then charged after it.

The kid spun and reached for the ball with his left foot, but Jacob had the better angle.

At the same time, the goalie was charging.

Jacob could have tried a shot, but out of the corner of his eye he saw a blue shirt racing in from the left.

He knocked the ball out to the open player. Only then did he see that it was Clayton, in perfect position.

POW!

The ball hit the net like a cannon ball.

And the score was tied.

Clayton jumped up and cheered. Then he

yelled, "We've got 'em now. One more, and it's all ours."

Jacob could feel it, too. This goal had been a team effort. Almost everyone had been involved. They had made great passes. Everyone was running to get open and they were rotating positions. That's what the coach was always talking about.

Total soccer.

One more time, and the championship belonged to Angel Park.

But the Springers weren't about to give the match away. Jackson yelled at his players, "Do you guys want Lindsay to get 'his' championship? We gotta stop him."

And suddenly the whole match came down to Jackson and Clayton again.

Jacob just hoped that Clayton wouldn't listen.

But it didn't take long to see that Clayton had decided to win the match himself again. The next time he got control of the ball, he dribbled straight up the field.

He went after Jackson with a couple of cuts and feints, and then he tried to charge past him.

Jackson played it cool. He held his square position, and then he got a foot on the ball. It popped free, and Clayton's momentum carried him by.

Jackson knocked the ball upfield and then chased it down. Metzger charged up alongside him, and the two made a run. Tammy was caught between the two. Trenton Daynes raced in to help out.

Tammy and Trenton managed to slow the attack, and some of the other Pride players caught up. Jacob thought they had the Springers bogged down enough to keep them from . . .

And then Jackson made an amazing play. He cut toward the goalpost, and Metzger fired a pass in his direction.

Tammy got in the way and knocked the pass down. It was a big save, and Jacob took a deep breath of relief.

But then Jackson somehow reversed his direction and darted around Tammy. He caught her from her blind side and took the ball away. Then he just pushed the ball into the net.

It all happened so fast it was hard to believe.

But the Springers had the lead again.

Coach Toscano yelled, "Teamwork. Teamwork. Clayton, you were trying to do it yourself."

But Clayton was almost frantic to get the match tied again. The only thing he seemed to think about was getting the ball and trying to save the day.

The more he kept the ball, the more he sucked the defense to him. And the more the Pride attack slowed down.

When it was all over, Clayton was still fighting for one last shot, and his teammates were watching in frustration.

The Pride had lost, and now they were back in a tie with the Kickers. That meant a play-off.

Jacob knew the Pride still had a chance to win. But the Kickers were tough.

And more than that, the Pride couldn't play the way they had today. If they did, the Kickers would destroy them.

Team Leader

The Angel Park players trudged off the field. It wasn't easy to listen to the Springers celebrate.

Parents came around and tried to make the Angel Park kids feel better, but the players knew that something was very wrong. It would take a big change to get the team playing the way it had a week earlier.

The coach talked about rotating positions and working together—total soccer—but no one seemed to be listening. They were all too disappointed. And some of the kids were mad.

Things were bad enough, but then, as the players stood up to leave, Tammy Hill said,

"Clayton, if you keep hogging the ball, we'll lose again."

Clayton exploded. He told Tammy she was an idiot, that she didn't know what she was talking about. "Without me, this team is nothing, and you know it. I'm the best player in this whole league."

He stomped away.

Jacob looked around at the players. Some of them were angry and were saying what they thought of Clayton. Others just looked really down. Jacob dropped down to the grass next to Nate, who had never gotten up.

"Oh, man," Nate said, "we're in big trouble now."

"I know," Jacob said.

Then Jacob heard his name being called. He looked up and saw the coach waving him over.

Jacob got up and walked over to the coach. "We didn't need that," Coach Toscano said.

"I know."

"Jacob, let me ask you something. Who, would you say, is our team leader?"

Jacob thought about that. "Nate and Heidi

are both leaders. But I think the one who has the biggest influence is probably Clayton."

"That's what I think, too. And when he leads in the right direction, we're a first-rate team."

The coach didn't have to say the rest. Jacob knew that Clayton was a bad influence right now.

"Jacob," the coach said, "somehow we have to get Clayton's attitude turned around. I've tried everything I know how to do, and he won't listen to me. So I'm thinking one of the players might have a better chance with him."

Jacob didn't like the sound of this. "Maybe Nate or Heidi—or both of them—should see what they can do."

"Actually, I'm thinking you might be the best one."

"Coach, Clayton *hates* me."

"No. I don't think so. I think he respects you. You've told him, straight out, that he's playing the game wrong right now. And deep down, he knows you're right."

Jacob shook his head. He didn't need this.

"Coach, I'm a new player. I'm only in fifth grade, and Clayton's in sixth."

"Jacob, you've improved more than anyone this year—so you have the players' respect. And that includes Clayton. I've thought about everyone on the team. I just think you can be honest and friendly with Clayton, and you can help him see that he's got to get his head on straight before this next match."

"How would I do that?"

"Just talk to him, I guess. Let him know that the whole team is depending on him."

Jacob just stood there. He was trying to think what in the world he could say to change Clayton's mind. If the coach couldn't do it, how could *he*?

"I'll give you one thing to think about."

Jacob looked up at the coach.

"Clayton hasn't been himself lately. He wasn't playing like this last week. Something seems to be bothering him."

Jacob remembered what Clayton had said to him after the match with the Racers. "He told me something sort of weird," Jacob said.

"I got the idea that he has some kind of trouble at home."

"Maybe you should talk to him about that."

Jacob didn't like the idea at all. But he said, "Okay. I guess I could see what I could do." But then he shook his head and said, "Don't expect any miracles."

Coach Toscano laughed his funny, loud, rolling laugh, and he patted Jacob on the shoulder. "I have faith in you," he said.

If only I had faith in myself, Jacob thought. But he didn't say that. He walked slowly back to Nate and Heidi.

They were sitting on the grass, waiting.

They both looked pretty depressed, especially Nate. "I can't believe we've come this far, and now we're letting everything get away from us," he said. But then he asked, "So what did the coach want?"

Jacob told them what they had talked about.

"How come you?" Nate asked.

"I don't know exactly." Jacob didn't want to give all of the coach's reasons. "But I need you guys to help me. What can I do?"

Nate just shook his head, but Heidi said,

"I think something is bugging Clayton. All of a sudden he thinks he has to be the big star every time. There must be some reason for that."

"Yeah. That's what the coach thinks, too," Jacob said. "I'm supposed to talk to him about that."

"Well, I hope you can say the right thing," Heidi said. "You didn't exactly show a lot of charm with him at practice the other day."

Heidi laughed, but Jacob didn't. He knew that was true, and he was scared. Maybe talking to Clayton would just make him angry again.

But then, it couldn't make things a whole lot worse.

So that night Jacob walked over to Clayton's house. Mrs. Lindsay answered the door. Her English accent was much stronger than Clayton's. "Yes, just a moment," she said, and then she called, "Clayton." The name sounded more like "Cly-tun" the way she said it.

In a few seconds Clayton came walking down the hallway from his room. When he saw Jacob, he stopped. "What do you want?" he said.

"Could I talk to you for a minute?"

Clayton seemed ready to say no, but his mother shot him a quick glance, and he said, "Okay. If you must." He turned and walked back to his room.

"Horrid manners!" his mother called after him.

When Jacob walked into the room, Clayton had already stretched out on his bed. "Go ahead. Talk. Then leave," he said. "And don't forget to tell me how I have to be a nice fellow in our next match, and pass the ball to all my teammates."

Jacob could see that he was in deep trouble before he even started. But he said, "Isn't that what they taught you in England?"

"Yes. Of course. But my teammates knew what to do with the ball once I passed it to them." He was staring straight at the ceiling.

"Don't we?"

Clayton sat up, suddenly. "Jacob, have you ever *seen* a real football match? Do you have any idea what the great players can do?"

"I've watched some World Cup matches on TV. And I've watched big league baseball, too. You can't expect a Little League team to play like professionals."

"That's not what I'm saying. I'm saying that kids our age in England could play circles around the teams here."

"Okay. I'm sure that's right. But we still have to use teamwork, don't we?"

"Never mind, Jacob. You wouldn't understand. Just leave me alone." He lay back on the bed.

Still, his voice had lost its hard edge. Jacob had the feeling that Clayton wanted to say something but couldn't bring himself to do it.

Jacob stood there for a long time, and then he took a chance. "How come your parents never come to the matches?"

Clayton didn't answer. He didn't move. But at least he didn't order Jacob out of the room. And he didn't say, "None of your business."

So Jacob waited.

Finally Clayton rolled over on his side. "Why do you ask that?" he said.

"I just wondered. I heard your dad was a soccer player. And I wondered why he didn't come to the matches. You said something the other day about my dad being there. So I just thought maybe . . ."

"Maybe what?"

"I don't know. Maybe that bothers you or something—that he doesn't come."

Clayton looked sad. For a time he didn't answer. Finally he said, "He says that football here is so bad he can't stand to watch it."

"Even if you're playing?"

Clayton nodded.

"I'll bet you'd like to have him come, wouldn't you?"

"Of course I would."

Some of the hardness had come back into Clayton's voice. Jacob thought maybe he had gotten into something he should have stayed away from.

And then he saw the last thing in the world he would have expected. Clayton had tears in his eyes.

★7★

Teamwork

Clayton turned his head and blinked, and then he quickly swiped his hand across his eyes. Jacob knew he was embarrassed. But Clayton swung his legs over the side of the bed, and he sat up. His voice was much softer when he said, "Jacob, nothing I do is enough for my father."

"What do you mean?"

"If I come home from a match and say we won, he laughs at me. 'I should think so,' he says. And if we lose, that's all the funnier. I tell him we have a pretty good team, and he says, 'Don't give me that. I've seen these Americans play.' "

"So do you feel like you've got to win every time?"

Clayton realized, finally, that Jacob was still standing. "Oh . . . uh . . . sit down," he said. He motioned to a chair in the corner.

Jacob walked over and sat down.

"It's not just winning. Every time I come home, he says, 'So how many goals did you score today?' I could say ten, and all he'd say was that the Americans don't know how to play defense. Once he even told me, 'You better be a big star in this country, because when we go back to England your days of glory will be all over.' "

"Maybe we're not quite so bad as he thinks. Maybe if he came to a match, he'd think we're pretty good."

"No way. He'd just laugh. He came a few times when we first got here, but after that I told him not to come if he was just going to make fun of us."

"I don't get it, Clayton. Why is he so hard on you?"

"I don't know. My mum says it's his way of trying to motivate me to work hard. I guess he thinks if I'm going to be any good, I have to work extra hard—since the competition is weak."

"Clayton, you know what I think?" Jacob said.

"What?"

"I think you should forget about your dad. A couple of weeks ago you were playing great, and so was the team. You were having a good time, too."

"I know. But that's when my father came home and told us we were going back to England next spring."

"What difference did that make?"

"I don't know." Clayton looked at the floor. "I guess I figured this was my last chance to do something big. I probably *won't* do very well in England."

"Maybe. Maybe not. But why not win the championship, and go home with that? That's the best memory you could have."

"That's what I was trying to do, Jacob. I never played so hard in my life. And all the coach did was get mad at me."

"Think about it, Clayton. You tried to take the ball all the way in and score by yourself.

Soccer doesn't work that way. You know that."

Clayton nodded. "But I just keep saying to myself, 'If I can't go right through these guys here, what will happen to me when I get home?' "

"Clayton, that doesn't make any sense. Nobody can keep the ball and dribble through a whole team—whether the team is English or American. You were trying to do something you can get away with once in a while, but after that, everyone collapses on you, and it won't work."

Clayton nodded again, as though he could finally admit that was true. "I *do* want the championship," he said.

"Okay. Let's get it."

And so they talked about what they could do. And the first thing was for Clayton to patch things up with the team.

"I don't know if I can do that," Clayton said.

"Just swallow your pride and—"

"It's not that. I think everyone hates me now."

"I don't think so. They got mad at you.

But if you tell them you're sorry, they'll listen."

Clayton looked at the floor for a time, and when he looked up, he nodded. "All right. I'll do it."

At practice next day he asked the coach if he could say something to the team. Jacob could tell that it took all his courage to face the players. But he did a good job.

"I was being the glory boy, I'm afraid," he told them. "I'm sorry about that. And I'm sorry about some of the things I said. I know I have to learn to control my mouth. But the important thing is, I do believe in total soccer. That's what we need to play on Thursday. And I'm ready to do it."

The players cheered.

Then Jacob got up and said, "Clayton just found out that he'll be going back to England before next season. So this is his last chance to win a championship here in the U.S. Let's give him something to take back. We never would have come this far without him!"

That brought a bigger cheer.

And a great practice followed.

Afterward, Coach Toscano talked to Jacob. "I knew I could count on you," he said. "But how did you do it?"

Jacob told the coach about the conversation he and Clayton had had. "I had a feeling it was something like that," the coach said. "But I'll tell you something, Jacob. His dad needs to watch Clayton play. He's a fine player. He'll do very well back in England."

Jacob was glad to hear that. "Will you do something for me, coach? Will you tell Clayton that? I think it would help him a lot."

"Okay," Coach Toscano said, "I'll tell him."

So the coach walked over to Clayton, and Jacob walked back to Heidi and Nate, who were waiting for him. "How did you do it?" Heidi was waiting to ask. "It was like a miracle. Did you see how Clayton played with us today?"

Jacob grinned, showing his funny split teeth. "I don't know. We just talked things out. Clayton's a good guy, really."

"He is today," Nate said. "He wasn't yesterday. Are you some sort of child genius?"

"Heck no. It was nothing like that. Do you really want to know what I did?"

"Sure."

"Well," Jacob said, very seriously, "I told him he better straighten up or I was going to knock his head off."

"What?" Heidi said.

"Yeah. It scared him bad. He begged me not to hurt him. So then I just told him what he was going to have to do to get me off his back."

By then Heidi knew she had been taken in. She suddenly punched Jacob a hard one on the shoulder. "Yeah, right. I'd have a better chance of scaring him than you would. You look like someone's little cocker spaniel."

"I know. But I'm *mean* when I get started."

Nate and Heidi laughed, and Jacob growled.

The important thing was, Clayton had not only changed his tune, he had changed the way he was playing in practice. Now, if he would only play that way in the play-off match.

Heidi said, "The Kickers are really playing well right now. I watched that match they had with the Bandits. They beat 'em a lot worse than we did."

Nate said, "Yeah. Since they lost that match with the Tornadoes, they've played a lot better. They knew we had to open the door for them to get back in. Once we did, they went crazy. I saw the Vandegraff brothers the other day, and they told me they *won't* lose to us."

"We beat them before," Jacob said.

"Yeah. But they've also beaten us," Heidi said.

"So what are you guys telling me?" Jacob said. "Don't you think we can win?"

"I'm not saying that. I think we *are* going to win," Heidi said. "I'm just telling you it's going to be a tough match."

And that Jacob did believe. But he wanted to win more than ever.

The next day the team got together again. But the coach wouldn't let them practice.

He brought out a whole cooler full of sodas. Then he said, "You need to have rested legs for tomorrow. And anyway, I have nothing else to teach you. If you play the way you did in practice yesterday, you'll be great."

"We'll wipe out the Kickers," Billy yelled.

But Coach Toscano said, "I didn't say that, Billy. I said that you'll be great. But the Kickers are good, too. Win or lose, we've had a great season."

And then a little smile broke across his face. "Of course, I'd rather win," he said.

"Let's make this a victory party," Heidi said. "Let's believe in ourselves. We can do it."

"Okay, fine," Coach Toscano said. "But what I want you to do is go to bed tonight and imagine yourself playing great soccer. Everyone working together. Everyone giving full effort all the time. If we can come somewhere close to that, we'll all have something to remember—something to make us happy all winter."

And Jacob liked the thought. The team had come a long way, and so had he. Now he wanted to play at the very top of his ability, and see all his friends do the same.

Then he smiled as he thought of what the coach had said. "Of course, I'd rather win," he'd said.

Yeah. Jacob agreed. He'd also rather win.

★8★

Play-off Match

That night Jacob lay awake for a long time just thinking about the big match. He was excited but not too worried. He was pretty sure the Pride would play well.

He was sort of amazed that he was just as excited now as he had been when the Angel Park Dodgers—his baseball team—had played for the Little League championship. He had always thought baseball would be his greatest love. But now, he cared just as much about soccer.

And the truth was, he was probably a little better at soccer than he was at baseball.

The next morning at breakfast, Jacob's mom teased him. "Well, Jacob, it's only a soccer match. It's not like *baseball*—your favorite sport."

Jacob only laughed. And then he suddenly began his other favorite pastime—pretending to be a sports announcer, or actually, *two* announcers. "Well, Hank," he said in a deep voice, "the Pride puts it all on the line this afternoon. Do you think Jacob Scott can lead his team to victory?"

"Shoot, Frank, there's no question about it. He's a two-sport star. And I suspect he'd be great at any sport he takes up. I hear he's thinking about getting into sumo wrestling next. Course, he needs to put on just a little weight."

Mom laughed at that one. "Hey, I don't think I want my kid to get into a sport where the guys leave their buns hanging out like that."

Dad had been eating all this time, and he seemed to be paying no attention. But now he looked up and said, "I don't know why not. The boy has cute buns. Just like his old man."

Everyone laughed at that—especially Jacob's sister.

But Jacob did want to set something straight. "I was just kidding about being a star. Our team has no stars today—not even Clayton. We're going to play *total soccer*. And that means everybody gets in on the action."

"Oh, no. Don't start that again," Jacob's sister said. Everyone laughed again. The Scotts had heard plenty about total soccer lately.

Jacob didn't care. All day at school that's what he kept thinking about—even when he should have had his mind on his school-work. By the time the match came that evening, he was so excited he couldn't stand still.

The whole team was the same way.

Across the field, Jacob could see that the Kickers were just as excited. But they were yelling and telling each other what they were going to do to the Pride.

The Pride players were sort of quiet. "Total soccer," they kept telling each other. "Keep the ball moving. Everyone plays together."

The match had been moved to the high school field so that enough seating would be available. And before the match started, an announcer told the big crowd that these two teams were both winners. They had tied for first place. Now they would play one last match for the championship.

Then he introduced every player, and

they ran out on the field one at a time. They were out there under the lights, and Jacob felt as though he were playing for the World Cup.

This was it!

The Kickers kicked off, and they came at the Pride as though they wanted to score on their very first possession.

But the Pride was ready. Their defense was all over the Kickers.

In fact, both teams were a little too excited, and for a while, not much happened. The defenses kept stopping the other team's attack.

Still, Jacob felt good about what he was seeing. Clayton was intense on defense. He was cutting off Peter Vandegraff, keeping him from getting the ball. He was also using his quickness to help other defenders.

When Clayton took control of the ball, he used his dribbling skills. But more than that, he was getting the ball to Lian or to the wings. And he was working with everyone else to get the ball into scoring position.

The only problem was that the Kickers' defense was *tough*. Their players were slashing in to cut off passes. They were stopping any deep penetration into their end of the field.

The battle was all taking place in the

middle of the field, and Jacob wondered what it was going to take to score. He knew his team was playing *hard,* but he didn't feel much sense of total soccer. The Kickers were breaking up the Pride attack and keeping the players off-balance.

Jacob had never run so hard in his life. He kept moving up to midfield, breaking and surging, trying to get clear for a pass. He was soon out of breath.

When the Kickers came on attack, Jacob marked a big fullback. The guy wasn't all that quick, but he was much taller and stronger than Jacob. Jacob really had to work to stay with him.

Halfway through the first half, neither team had scored, and the pace was finally starting to slow. Both teams were wearing down from all the hard running.

Jacob had a feeling something was about to give. What happened, however, wasn't quite what he had in mind.

Peter passed the ball to his brother, Klaus, faked to his left, and then cut behind Clayton.

Clayton was up on Peter, playing him close, and he got caught off-balance. Peter had a step on Clayton, and Klaus saw his chance. He kicked a wall pass—the give-and-go play—and got the ball back to Peter.

Peter dribbled straight ahead for the goal. But Clayton made up the distance quickly. He reached in and knocked the ball away.

Peter had to break off his run and chase down the ball, and he took control again.

Clayton now had time to get between Peter and the goal. He stepped in to make a tackle.

Peter was slick though. He swung hard at the ball, as though he were passing, but he stopped his leg at the last second. Then he tapped the ball a few inches to his left.

Clayton took the fake and looked to see where the pass was going.

Just that quickly, Peter reached out with his left foot, pulled the ball back, tapped it out to the right, and then broke past Clayton.

Suddenly Peter was in the clear. He rushed at the goal.

Nate had seen the whole thing. He burst ahead, straight at Peter.

That's when Peter lifted a little blooper of a shot, right over Nate's head.

Nate jumped for it and almost got a hand on it. But the ball bounced behind him and rolled toward the goal.

Nate spun, took a quick step, and dove. His fingers touched the ball, but he couldn't quite get hold of it.

It rolled into the net.

Score!

Jacob felt his stomach knot. In a match like this, one goal could win it.

Still, that wasn't what worried him the most.

Peter had beaten Clayton. And Clayton wouldn't like that. When he got mad at himself, he usually tried to get a score himself—to make up for his mistake.

That's the one thing the Pride didn't need today.

Jacob ran over to Clayton. "We'll get it back," he said.

Clayton was tired, the same as everyone else. He was leaning down to catch his breath. "What a play!" he said. "Peter is really something."

Jacob wasn't sure how to read that. At least Clayton wasn't getting down on himself.

And after the kickoff, and some battling back and forth, Clayton got the ball with a little room to move. He pushed the ball straight at Peter.

Jacob was pretty sure that Clayton would try to show Peter what *he* could do.

Clayton dribbled ahead, under control. The two players were watching each other like a pair of boxers waiting to throw a punch.

And then, suddenly, Clayton turned on the speed. Peter was on him tight, and Klaus slipped in to double him.

The Vandegraff boys knew that Clayton was going for it, and they both went after him.

But Clayton suddenly broke off his run, stepped over the ball, and stopped it. Then he dropped the ball to Sterling, who had come up from his fullback position.

"Lian, cover," Clayton yelled. Lian slipped back into a defensive position and let Sterling go on through.

The two Vandegraffs had been drawn in by Clayton. Now Sterling was ahead of both of them and driving up the field.

Patty Pinelli came over from the wing to slow Sterling down, but when she did, Henry was open on the wing.

Sterling hit him with a lead pass, and Henry angled toward the goal.

Heidi faked a move toward Henry, but then she stopped and cut behind the fullback who was covering her.

Henry saw the move, and he kicked under the ball and arched it toward the goalpost—right where Heidi was heading.

The pass was a little short. Heidi leaped, but she had the wrong angle to head the ball into the net.

The pass had pulled the goalie and two defenders toward the ball. Heidi saw her chance to head the ball back to Jacob, who was moving in from the left, toward the goal.

Jacob got the ball but had a crowd in front of him. Without a second's hesitation he slapped the ball over to Sterling, who was still coming hard up the middle.

Sterling took a big swing with his leg but only faked a hard shot.

The goalie and a fullback both reacted to the left.

And then Sterling shoved the ball into the right corner.

It was *beautiful*.

Perfect!

The whole team clustered around Sterling and slapped him on the back. But they all had worked the ball and they all had gotten the score.

Total soccer.

★9★

Now or Never

Things were starting to work for the Pride. They were moving the ball better all the time. But they couldn't get another score.

The half ended 1 to 1.

So it all came down to the final half of the final match.

The coach didn't have much to say at halftime. Mostly he congratulated them.

"Your defense was great," he told them. "And your attack is coming together. You're rotating and shifting. Every player is a danger that way. The Kickers can't focus on Clayton or anyone else. If they do, someone else will make them pay."

And it was true.

Jacob felt the flow of those last few minutes. That's how soccer was supposed to feel. It wasn't broken up like baseball. It was all one motion when it was right.

But the Kickers were playing well, too. A mistake or two on either side would probably decide the victory.

The coach let the kids spend most of the time resting. Heidi lay back on the grass and said, "I love playing soccer like that. That goal we got was beautiful."

"You should have seen the defense," Nate said. "Everyone was covering and switching off. Klaus made a great play, but we really didn't make any big mistakes."

When the team got up to go back on the field, Clayton told everyone, "Hey, let's do it. Let's keep up the pressure both ways, and we'll get 'em. All together."

The players ran back to the field. And the flow was still there. For a time, the break wouldn't come, but the attack was moving the ball, creating shots, and the defense was unbeatable. The Kickers weren't even getting any shots on goal.

Then Tammy stole a pass in Pride territory and quickly flipped the ball over to Billy.

The whole team yelled, *"Attack!"*

Jacob wanted to get himself clear. He started working on it early, while the ball was still well down the field.

He ran, sort of slowly, to the left wing, taking a defender with him. And then he slowed even more and pretended to be breathing hard.

Chris took the ball down the touchline until he got cut off. He passed back to Trenton. Trenton dribbled toward the center of the field and hit Jared, who was in the game at fullback instead of goalie.

Things seemed to be getting bogged down in the center, with no one to take a pass.

Jacob watched and played a waiting game. He stood at the edge of the field, and he kept breathing hard.

Just then Chris broke up the field.

Jared saw his chance, and he kicked a long pass up the touchline.

It looked as though the ball might go out of bounds, but Chris leaped and headed the ball inside the touchline. Then he came down and trapped the ball himself.

Jacob was still hanging back, and his defender suddenly realized that Chris was ahead of his man and would have an open path toward the goal.

Jacob's defender rushed at Chris, and Jacob had his chance.

He charged toward the goal, and Chris saw him all the way. Chris dribbled across the field and looked to pass. But no defender was behind Jacob. It would be an offside pass.

Jacob saw the same thing and angled backward, enough to get beyond a fullback, who was dropping back.

Instantly, Chris drove a pass to Jacob, but he led him a little too much.

Jacob chased after the ball and got it. He turned to get a shot, but the fullback had come over to take him.

The guy reached in and knocked the ball away.

Jacob dashed back to the ball, but he was guarded closely now.

And Brian, who had come all the way up the field from his sweeper position, surged past his defender. Jacob slid a little pass across the grass to him.

Brian, like a forward, whipped his leg at

the ball, hit it with the top of his shoe, and *drove* it at the goal.

The goalie had almost no time to react, but he shot a leg out and managed to kick the ball off to the side.

Jacob's heart sank.

But then he saw Clayton slashing toward the ball.

His angle was all wrong. The ball was outside the goal area, bouncing toward the goal line.

But Clayton leaped like a long jumper. He turned all the way around in the air and swept the ball with his left foot, back toward the goal.

He couldn't get off a shot, but he kept the ball alive and in the middle.

And Heidi was there.

She took the ball right out of the air and volleyed a *blazing* shot into the net.

Score!

The Pride players went crazy. They pounded on Heidi and Clayton, but then they didn't know where to stop. Everyone had gotten in the act. And so the whole team turned into a little mob in front of the goal.

They were all bouncing up and down at the same time, clinging to each other.

"That's what I call *soccer!*" Clayton was screaming. "Let's keep it up!"

Finally the celebration broke up. About then, Jacob heard one of the Kickers yell, "Who let Scott get loose? Who was marking him, anyway?"

The wing who had been marking Jacob spun around and said, "I *had* to leave him. That side was wide open. Patty's the one who got beat."

"Never mind!" Klaus yelled. "Let's just get a goal and tie it up." But he sounded mad, too.

Jacob could see that the Pride had the match.

About two minutes later, Clayton stole the ball from Peter and spotted Adam Snarr cutting across the middle. He hit Adam, and Adam dropped the ball off to Tanya.

Tanya slowed for a moment, and then she turned on the speed to get past her defender.

Clayton was burning up the field, and he caught up with Tanya.

She dropped the ball over to Clayton.

Clayton had a breakaway, and he couldn't pass without being offside.

So he dribbled hard at the goalie.

The goalie came out to meet him, and Clayton made the move of a lifetime. He knocked his dribble out to the right, cut to the ball, and stepped around it. His back was to the goalie. He flipped the ball into the air, as though he were juggling, but lifted it out to his own left.

And then he leaped, twisting in the air and stretching out flat. He drove a hard shot around the goalie.

Slam!

3 to 1.

And the Pride was not finished.

The Kickers were blaming each other and getting mad. The Pride was as smooth as a flowing stream.

When Clayton stole the ball again and drove into Kickers' territory, the whole team seemed to collapse on him. They knew what he could do if they left him one-on-one with any player.

But so many got pulled in, that Jacob was left wide open.

Someone did manage to kick the ball off

Clayton's shins, but it bounced high in the air. Clayton reacted first, and he got up to head the ball.

He hit the ball right to Jacob, who was all alone.

Jacob reacted without thinking. What had been so tough for him early in the season was like an instinct now. He trapped the ball, pushed his weight forward over the ball, drove his foot through the ball, and landed on his shooting foot.

The shot was a cannon blast, low and into the corner.

The goalie didn't even make a move for it. He watched it hit the net and then he collapsed on the ground.

4 to 1, and everyone knew the match was over.

After that, the Kickers played more defense than attack, as though they had given up all hope of winning and just wanted to keep the score from getting any worse.

And then the final whistle blew.

The fullback who had been marking Jacob grabbed his shoulder and said, "You guys are great. You deserved to win."

Jacob thanked him and then ran to his teammates, who had all headed for Clayton. The whole team ended up piled in one big mass of arms and legs. Jacob jumped on top.

After some wild screaming and cheering, kids started rolling off and then running around and jumping, as though they couldn't think what else to do.

Heidi grabbed Jacob and hugged him, and the two jumped up and down together for a while. And then Nate found them and they turned into a three-part jumping jack.

"What do you think of soccer now?" Heidi yelled into Jacob's ear.

Jacob grinned. "It's not too bad," he said. "Not too bad."

At the same time Nate was saying, "I've always wanted to play on a good team. And this is a *great* one."

Clayton finally got up, and he started slapping hands with everyone. "Who says we can't play soccer in this country?" he said. "I'll tell my friends in England about this team."

And that's when Coach Toscano, who had been standing back, walked into the crazy crowd. "Kids, you played a *brilliant* match," he said.

The kids tried to get Coach Toscano up on their shoulders. But they botched it and ended up dropping him on the grass. He only laughed.

Finally things slowed down, and the announcer asked the kids to line up for their trophies. One at a time, the players stepped forward and got their awards, and then they lined up again to slap hands with the Kickers.

By then the parents were coming out to congratulate the players and hug their own kids.

That's when Jacob noticed that Clayton was standing all by himself. Jacob couldn't think what to do. Hadn't his parents come? Not even to the championship?

For the first time, Clayton stopped smiling, and he suddenly looked very much alone.

Jacob pulled his own parents over. He wanted to have someone there to tell Clayton how great he had played.

But it was the coach who got there first.

"Clayton," he said. "I had a guy tape the game tonight. I want you to take the tape home. And I want you to make your dad watch it."

"He'll just tell me that in England, we would have—"

"No, Clayton. No. You can play with English boys. You're not just good; you're *very* good. You could even play in *Brazil!*"

Clayton laughed and thanked the coach. And he took the tape. "I'll show it to him," he said. "And I'll take it home to England and show all my friends."

Jacob liked that. Maybe Americans could play this game after all.

Final League Standings

Kickers	9–3
Pride	9–3
Tornadoes	7–5
Springers	6–6
Racers	5–7
Bandits	4–8
Gila Monsters	2–10

Match 12 Scores:

Pride	9	Gila Monsters	1
Racers	3	Springers	2
Tornadoes	2	Kickers	1
Bandits	bye		

Match 13 Scores:

Pride	5	Racers	3
Bandits	6	Springers	3
Kickers	7	Gila Monsters	0
Tornadoes	bye		

Match 14 Scores:

Springers	3	Pride	2
Kickers	5	Bandits	1
Gila Monsters	3	Tornadoes	1
Racers	bye		

Championship Playoff

Pride	4	Kickers	1

Angel Park Soccer Strategies

Soccer, like football and basketball, is a game of game plans, of strategies. Both professionals and amateurs use strategies to give themselves a general sense of what to do *as a team*. Without teamwork and strategy, soccer games would only be a bunch of people running around a field, kicking a ball back and forth.

This is why players have particular jobs to do, either scoring goals or defending against goals. This makes the game more interesting— and more challenging. When a player is running upfield with the ball, he will almost always be cut off before he scores a goal himself. This is why players learn strategies. When the time comes, they'll know what to do. They'll know where their teammates are without even looking.

Or at least that's the idea. The success of the strategies depends on the skill of the players. The strategies we've presented here, in these diagrams, are standard game plans that the Angel Park Pride might attempt to use in a game. If you think your team could profit from a little strategic thinking, show these to your coach. Give them a try. Good luck!

Kickoff

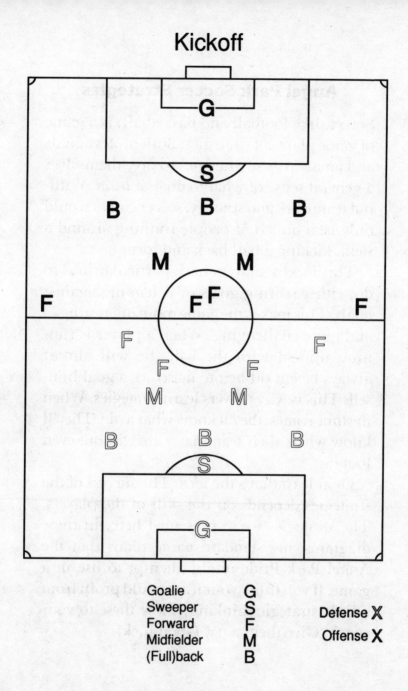

Goalie	G	
Sweeper	S	**Defense** X
Forward	F	
Midfielder	M	**Offense** X
(Full)back	B	

94

Throw-in at Midfield, Stage #1

Goalie	**G**
Sweeper	**S**
Forward	**F**
Midfielder	**M**
(Full)back	**B**

Offense **X** Defense **X̶**
Ball **O**
Player movement ——————→
Pass ------→
Throw ---·---·→

Throw-in at Midfield, Stage #2

Goalie	G
Sweeper	S
Forward	F
Midfielder	M
(Full)back	B

Offense X   Defense X
Ball   O
Pass   ------->
Shot   ·············>

Throw-in in Offensive End #1
"Long Throw"

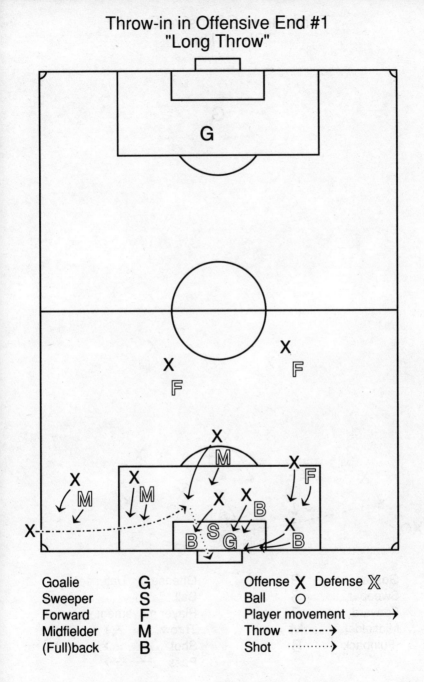

Goalie	**G**	Offense **X** Defense **X**	
Sweeper	**S**	Ball ○	
Forward	**F**	Player movement ——→	
Midfielder	**M**	Throw ·–·–·→	
(Full)back	**B**	Shot ·······→	

Throw-in in Offensive End #2
"Short Throw"

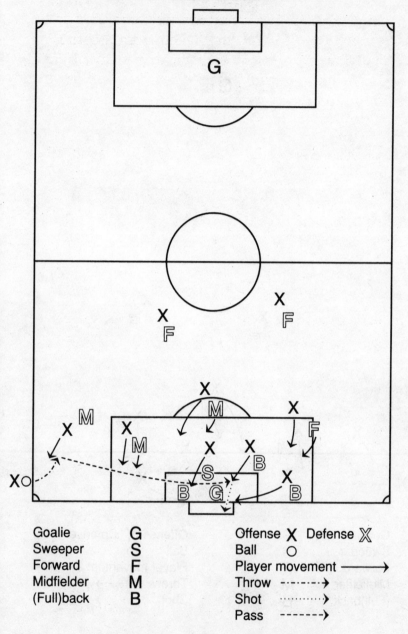

Goalie	**G**	Offense **X**	Defense **X**
Sweeper	**S**	Ball	**O**
Forward	**F**	Player movement	———→
Midfielder	**M**	Throw	·—·—·→
(Full)back	**B**	Shot	········→
		Pass	------→

Glossary

corner kick   A free kick taken from a corner area by a member of the attacking team, after the defending team has propelled the ball out-of-bounds across the goal line.

cover   A defensive maneuver in which a player places himself between an opponent and the goal.

cross pass   A pass across the field, often toward the center, intended to set up the shooter.

cutting   Suddenly changing directions while dribbling the ball in order to deceive a defender.

direct free kick   An unimpeded shot at the goal, awarded to a team sustaining a major foul.

dribbling   Maneuvering the ball at close range with only the feet.

feinting   Faking out an opponent with deceptive moves.

forwards   Players whose primary purpose is to score goals. Also referred to as "strikers."

free kick   A direct *or* indirect kick awarded to a team, depending on the type of foul committed by the opposing team.

fullbacks   Defensive players whose main purpose is to keep the ball out of the goal area.

goalkeeper The ultimate defender against attacks on the goal, and the only player allowed to use his hands.

halfbacks See Midfielders.

heading Propelling the ball with the head, especially the forehead.

indirect free kick A shot at the goal involving at least two players, awarded to a team sustaining a minor foul.

juggling A drill using the thighs, feet, ankles, or head to keep the ball in the air continuously.

kickoff A center place kick which starts the action at the beginning of both the first and second halves or after a goal has been scored.

marking Guarding a particular opponent.

midfielders Players whose main purpose is to get the ball from the defensive players to the forwards. Also called "halfbacks."

penalty kick A direct free kick awarded to a member of the attacking team from a spot 12 yards in front of the goal. All other players must stay outside the penalty area except for the goalie, who must remain stationary until the ball is in play.

punt   A drop kick made by the goalkeeper.

shooting   Making an attempt to score a goal.

strikers   See Forwards.

sweeper   The last player, besides the goal-keeper, to defend the goal against attack.

tackling   Stealing the ball from an opponent by using the feet or a shoulder charge.

total soccer   A system by which players are constantly shifting positions as the team shifts from offense to defense. Also called "position-less soccer."

volley kick   A kick made while the ball is still in the air.

wall   A defensive barrier of players who stand in front of the goal area to aid the goalkeeper against free kicks.

wall pass   This play involves a short pass from one teammate to another, followed by a return pass to the first player as he runs past the defender. Also called the "give-and-go."

wingbacks   Outside fullbacks.

wingers   Outside forwards.

DEAN HUGHES has written many books for children, including the popular *Nutty* stories and *Jelly's Circus*. He has also published such works of literary fiction for young adults as the highly acclaimed *Family Pose*. Writing keeps Mr. Hughes very busy, but he does find time to run and play golf—and he loves to watch almost all sports. His home is in Utah. He and his wife have three children, all in college.

READ THESE OTHER ANGEL

#1 MAKING THE TEAM

Kenny, Harlan, and Jacob have officially made the team, but some of the older players—mostly team bully Rodney Bunson—seem bent on making life miserable for the three rookies. Can the third-grade Little Leaguers stand up to some big-league bullying?

#2 BIG BASE HIT

Awkward and big for his age, Harlan seems to do everything wrong—and it's making him wonder whether he really belongs on the team at all. But then the pitcher throws the ball, and Harlan gives the team just what they've all been waiting for: a big base hit!

#3 WINNING STREAK

Kenny's in a slump—and it spells big trouble for the undefeated Angel Park Dodgers. Jacob's got a few tricks that he thinks will help, but his wacky ideas only seem to make matters worse. Then he hits on the one trick that puts Kenny back in action, just in time to put the team back on a winning streak!

#4 WHAT A CATCH!

Brian desperately wants to make his last season in Little League his best ever, but his mistakes might cost the team the championship. The All-Stars try to help their nervous friend build his self-confidence, but it takes a pep talk from a major-league pro to get Brian back on track.